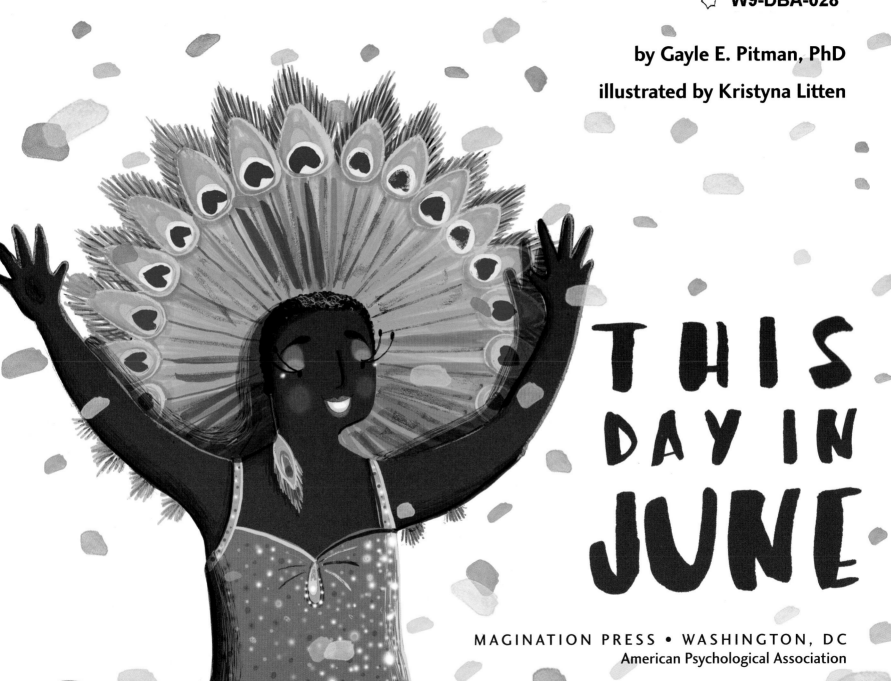

by Gayle E. Pitman, PhD

illustrated by Kristyna Litten

THIS DAY IN JUNE

MAGINATION PRESS • WASHINGTON, DC
American Psychological Association

This day in June
Parade starts soon!

Rainbow arches
Joyful marches

**Motors roaring
Spirits soaring**

Voices chanting
Doggies panting

Clad in leather
Perfect weather

Artists painting
Sisters sainting

Banners swaying
Children playing

Dancers jumping
Music pumping

Sidewalk shaking
Tummies aching

Painted ladies
Crying babies

Fancy dresses
Flowing tresses

Loving kisses
So delicious

All invited
All excited

Reading Guide

For an explanation of the images and allusions in the book, as well as more information about lesbian, gay, bisexual, and transgender (LGBT) history and culture, read on.

This day in June/Parade starts soon! — Although pride celebrations can be held anytime during the year, they are traditionally held in June to commemorate the Stonewall riots. On the morning of June 28, 1969, police conducted a routine raid at the Stonewall Inn, which was a gay bar in Greenwich Village, New York. It was common during that time period for gay bars to be raided by the police. That night in June was different, however—patrons of the bar fought back against the police and resisted arrest, which led to a three-day protest now known as the Stonewall riots. The Stonewall riots are considered to mark the beginning of the gay liberation movement.

Rainbow arches/Joyful marches — The rainbow flag is commonly associated with the LGBT community. People may wear a rainbow flag symbol as a way of identifying themselves as a member or an ally of the LGBT community. They may also wear the rainbow as a symbol of pride. The LGBT community is very diverse, and the rainbow flag reflects that diversity. Each color of the rainbow represents a different element: red (life), orange (healing), yellow (sunlight), green (nature), blue (serenity or harmony), and purple (spirit).

Motors roaring/Spirits soaring — Most pride parades start with a contingent of lesbians riding motorcycles, called the Dykes on Bikes. Lesbians have long been associated with motorcycles, sometimes as a stereotype, and sometimes as a symbol of feminism and visibility. Usually the word "dyke" is considered to be a derogatory term; however, the gay and lesbian community has a long history of reclaiming negative terms and using them within the LGBT community. The word "gay," for example, was at one time considered to be derogatory, but now is very commonly used.

Voices chanting/Doggies panting — Because people who are gay, lesbian, bisexual, and transgender (LGBT) have faced discrimination, there has been a long history of activism in the LGBT community. In the 1960s and 1970s, people who are LGBT fought to remove "homosexuality" as a psychiatric diagnosis from the *Diagnostic and Statistical Manual of Mental Disorders* (DSM). In June 1972, Queens school teacher Jeanne Manford marched with her gay son, Morty, in New York's Christopher Street Liberation Day March, the precursor to today's pride parades. The enthusiastic reactions she received led her—along with her husband and other gay rights activists, families, and allies—to create PFLAG, the nation's largest organization for parents, families, friends, and straight allies united with LGBT people to move equality forward. With its mission of support, education, and advocacy, PFLAG recently celebrated its 40th anniversary. In the 1980s, groups like the AIDS Coalition to Unleash Power (ACT-UP) formed to raise awareness about the impact of HIV and AIDS on the gay community. Throughout the 1990s and 2000s, the LGBT community worked to repeal Don't Ask Don't Tell, the military policy that prevented people who were openly gay or lesbian from serving in the military. More recently, the LGBT community has started to win decades-long battles for legal recognition of same-sex marriage and workplace

fairness. Pride celebrations typically have an element of political awareness and activism.

Clad in leather/Perfect weather — The association between gay men and leather originated in the post-WWII era. It provided an alternative to the image that stereotyped gay men as feminine. Leather also provided a symbol of visibility for gay men. In the 1950s, it was generally not safe for people to be openly gay, and thus the leather jacket became a way for gay men to identify other gay men. Later, leather became associated with the lesbian community, mainly as an expression of feminism.

Artists painting/Sisters sainting — The Sisters of Perpetual Indulgence is a group of artists, activists, and self-described nuns for the queer community that formed in San Francisco in 1979. The Sisters organized primarily to advocate safe-sex practices and to help AIDS patients when other social service or community groups would not. The group is devoted to community service and outreach and to promoting human rights and respect for diversity.

Banners swaying/Children playing — Like the rainbow flag, the pink triangle is a familiar symbol in the gay and lesbian community. During the

Holocaust, gay men and lesbians were imprisoned and forced to wear arm badges with symbols identifying the group they belonged to. Jewish people wore the Star of David, gay men wore a downward-pointing pink triangle, and lesbian women wore a downward-pointing black triangle. Now, members of the LGBT community may wear the pink triangle as a symbol of pride.

Dancers jumping/Music pumping — The arts have always been an integral part of gay culture, and same-sex love and gender-bending themes have found their way into the arts for centuries. For example, cross-dressing and playing with gender expression were common themes in a number of Shakespeare's plays, including *Twelfth Night* and *As You Like It*. During the 1950s, when it was not safe to identify publicly as gay or lesbian, many gay men sought expression in musical theater. Gay men have also been drawn to the dance world, as well as to a wide variety of other creative and artistic endeavors. In a culture that is largely homophobic, many LGBT people have found a welcoming and accepting environment in the arts.

Sidewalk shaking/Tummies aching — Since the 1990s, more lesbian and gay couples have chosen to become parents. While many lesbians and gay men parent children from previous heterosexual relationships, many same-sex couples are choosing to have children of their own. Lesbian couples may choose to have a child through donor insemination, while gay male couples may have a child by using a surrogate. Another possibility available to gay and lesbian couples is adoption. However, not every state allows same-sex couples to adopt children, and not every state grants parenting rights to non-biological parents. Children of Lesbians and Gays Everywhere (COLAGE) is a resource for people who have a lesbian, gay, bisexual, or transgender parent. In addition to numerous web-based resources, COLAGE has chapters in several major and mid-sized cities throughout the United States. In addition, the Gay-Straight Alliance Network helps connect school-based gay–straight alliances (GSAs) together, and provides resources and support to them. It also provides resources to teens who wish to start a GSA in their own schools.

Painted ladies/Crying babies — San Francisco is well known for being a gay mecca. The Castro, a district in San Francisco, is the largest gay neighborhood in the world. San Francisco was also home to Harvey Milk, the first openly gay man to be elected to public office in California. The "painted ladies" refers to a row of colorful Victorian houses overlooking Alamo Square, a neighborhood in San Francisco.

Fancy dresses/Flowing tresses — Many pride parades have a very festive, almost Mardi Gras–like character. It's common to see highly elaborate floats, over-the-top musical performances, and drag queens dressed in an exaggerated feminine style. The flamboyance and theatricality associated with pride parades have been controversial, as some critics within the LGBT population think it portrays the LGBT community as outlandish. However, most people in the LGBT community see these qualities as part of the celebratory nature of the event.

Loving kisses/So delicious — Since the 1990s, same-sex couples have been fighting for the right to marry. The U.S. government passed a law in 1996 called the Defense of Marriage Act (DOMA), which defined marriage as being between a man and a woman. Some states have defined marriage as being between a man and a woman, while other states have legalized same-sex marriage. Still other states allow same-sex couples to enter into domestic partnerships or civil unions. A lot of activist efforts

in the gay and lesbian community currently focus on marriage equality. Human Rights Campaign (HRC) has been active in these efforts. HRC advocates on behalf of LGBT Americans, mobilizes grassroots actions in diverse communities, invests strategically to elect fair-minded individuals to office, and educates the public about LGBT issues including the right for same-sex couples to get married. Marriage equality activists won a huge victory in June 2013, when the Supreme Court ruled that DOMA was unconstitutional and dismissed Proposition 8, a California ballot proposition and state constitutional amendment outlawing same-sex marriage.

Note to Parents and Caregivers

Today, people who are lesbian, gay, bisexual, or transgender (LGBT) experience higher levels of acceptance and visibility than ever before. While most parents in same-sex relationships are used to fielding questions about their families, many heterosexual parents don't talk to their children at all about sexual orientation or gender identity. Many heterosexual parents want to talk to their children about sexual orientation, believing that prejudice and discrimination against LGBT people are wrong, but may feel as if they lack the tools to have these conversations.

HOW THIS BOOK CAN HELP

This Day In June provides a positive, normalizing, and exuberant reflection of the LGBT community, and can serve as a jumping-off point for children to ask questions about sexual orientation and gender identity. It's important for *all* parents to talk with their kids about sexual orientation and gender variance for a variety of reasons, including:

- Talking about LGBT people in a positive way normalizes all sexual and gender identities. This normalization helps inoculate your child against ignorance and fear—common precursors to prejudice, bullying, and violence against children whose behavior or expression challenges traditional gender norms.
- Bringing up these issues proactively will convey that you believe in acceptance, respect, and understanding. In contrast, your silence could be misinterpreted as discomfort or intolerance.
- Talking to your kids directly about sexual orientation provides them with correct and positive information, and prevents the spread of misinformation and inaccurate beliefs.
- Promoting acceptance of LGBT people helps to reduce sexism. Homophobia and sexism are inextricably linked; LGBT people challenge traditional gender roles and sexist attitudes. If you believe in gender equality, talking to your child about lesbian, gay, bisexual, and transgender people is one way of combating sexism.
- Conversations such as this pave the way for a smoother coming-out experience for your child, if your child is gay (and that possibility might not be evident right away).

TALKING TO CHILDREN

How children process these conversations will depend on their age and their cognitive maturity level. Here are some tips for talking to children about sexual orientation and gender identity in age-appropriate ways.

3-5 years old:

- Let them ask questions. Young children are naturally observant and curious, and this is an opportunity to support those qualities. At this age, children tend to ask questions in order to satisfy curiosity, and rarely as a way of conveying an implicit value judgment.
- Keep answers simple and concrete. For example, if your child asks why her classmate has two daddies but no mommy, you can say, "Some children have two daddies, and some have two mommies. Her daddies love each other just like I love your daddy (or mommy)." Some of the illustrations in *This Day In June* involve two same-sex adults kissing or holding hands, and this can be an opportunity to provide a concrete example to your child.
- Don't think that you have to make the conversation about sex. Sometimes parents fear talking about sexual orientation with young children because they're afraid their children will ask about sex. Children in this age range aren't typically thinking about sex at all. If this question does come up—for example, if your child asks how two daddies have a baby—find a book that's applicable to all types of families for talking about how babies are made.
- If your child likes pretending to be the opposite sex, or if your child is engaging in play behavior associated with the opposite sex, let him do so—it's common, normal, and healthy for kids to do this. In *This Day In June*, there are several examples of cross-gender dress, and this can be normalized to your child as a fun way of playing and expressing oneself. Preventing a child from engaging in opposite-sex play—for example, by telling a boy he shouldn't play with that doll—conveys to the child that cross-gender behavior is unhealthy and inappropriate. This can limit the range of skills and interests that children develop as they mature, regardless of their gender identity.

6-12 years old:

- At this age, a child might not be asking questions just to satisfy curiosity. Try to understand why your child is bringing up these issues. Did a classmate call another kid a "fag," or say, "You're gay!" in a taunting manner? Did a group of children make fun of your child's friend, because that friend has two moms? Your child might need reassurance and tips on how to navigate these situations with peers.

- Children in this age range are likely to develop close friendships with same-sex peers—and sometimes they can get teased by others for this. If your child gets teased, listen to her feelings and concerns, and help her come up with strategies to handle these social situations. This may also be an opportunity for you to speak with school personnel about these behaviors.
- Bullying and name-calling are likely to start within this age range. If your child is engaging in these behaviors, this is a good time to reinforce to your child the importance of acceptance and respect. It's also helpful to find out why your child is behaving this way. Children in the older end of this age range become very concerned about peer acceptance. Your child may think that making fun of someone who's different is a way to gain the respect of their peers. Challenge this idea with your child, and discuss how it may actually achieve the opposite.
- If your child is questioning whether he is gay or gender-variant, reassure him that the answer will become clear in time, and that you love him no matter what his sexual orientation, gender identity, or gender expression. This might also be a good time for you to identify resources in the LGBT community that might be helpful to your child.

- If you don't know the answer to a question about sexual orientation or gender identity, say so—and work with your child to find the answers together.

13–18 years old:

- It's critical to understand that, at this age, peer acceptance is of the utmost importance. For example, teens who have two moms or two dads may not want to advertise that fact to their friends. Keep the lines of conversation open at home, but allow your teen to exercise some independence and make her own choices about how to handle these situations.
- Sexual orientation and gender identity often become apparent in adolescence. If your child says, "I'm gay," listen carefully, and convey your support, love, and acceptance. This is often easier to do if you've been talking with your child about sexual orientation from an early age.
- Maintain awareness of your teen's school and community environment. Although some high schools have gay–straight alliances, many do not—and many high school environments are chilly to LGBT teens. Without support from family, peers,

and their school, LGBT teens are at risk for poor academic performance, drug use, depression, and suicidal behaviors. Regardless of whether your teen is heterosexual, gay, lesbian, bisexual, or transgender, try to help cultivate resources in your teen's school and community that provide support for LGBT people.

- Teenagers are naturally interested in political and social issues. Talking with your teen about marriage equality, parenting rights, employment discrimination, and religious views about LGBT people can potentially lead to rich conversations. The Reading Guide in *This Day In June* can be extremely helpful in these discussions.
- Seek support and community with other LGBT parents and with heterosexual allies. It takes a village— as the saying goes—to provide a welcoming and accepting environment for LGBT teens.

About the Author

Gayle E. Pitman, PhD is a professor of psychology and women's studies at Sacramento City College. Her teaching and writing focuses on gender and sexual orientation, and she has worked extensively with the lesbian, gay, bisexual, and transgender (LGBT) community.

About the Illustrator

Kristyna Litten studied illustration at Edinburgh College of Art. Kristyna is influenced by books and animation from Eastern Europe which has led to a fascination for illustrating and writing her own picture books full of loveable characters and charming narratives. She prefers to draw quickly to give an energetic line quality to her illustrations, often adding color and other hand-produced textures digitally.

About Magination Press

Magination Press is an imprint of the American Psychological Association, the largest scientific and professional organization representing psychologists in the United States and the largest association of psychologists worldwide.

About the American Psychological Association

The American Psychological Association (APA) is committed to applying the science and practice of psychology to the fundamental problems of human welfare and the promotion of equitable and just treatment of all segments of society through education, training, and public policy.

To all of the courageous pioneers in the LGBT community who helped to make Pride what it is today – GP

For Kirsty and James – KL

Published by

MAGINATION PRESS
An Educational Publishing Foundation Book
American Psychological Association
750 First Street, NE
Washington, DC 20002

For more information about our books, including a complete catalog, please write to us, call 1-800-374-2721, or visit our website at www.apa.org/pubs/magination.

Book design by Susan White
Printed by Phoenix Color Corporation, Hagerstown, MD
Logos, images, and phrases relating to Human Rights Campaign (HRC) or Parents, Families and Friends of Lesbians and Gays, Inc. (PFLAG) have been reproduced with permission.

Library of Congress Cataloging-in-Publication Data
Pitman, Gayle E.
This day in June / by Gayle E. Pitman ; illustrated by Kristyna Litten.
    pages cm
"American Psychological Association."
Summary: "A picture book illustrating a Pride parade. The endmatter serves as a primer on LGBT history and culture and explains the references made in the story"—Provided by publisher.
ISBN-13: 978-1-4338-1658-1 (hardcover)
ISBN-10: 1-4338-1658-X (hardcover)
ISBN-13: 978-1-4338-1659-8 (pbk.)
ISBN-10: 1-4338-1659-8 (pbk.)
[1. Stories in rhyme. 2. Gay pride parades—Fiction. 3. Parades—Fiction.]
I. Litten, Kristyna, illustrator. II. Title.
PZ8.3.P5586836Th 2013
[E]—dc23   2013021623

Manufactured in the United States of America
10 9 8 7 6 5 4 3